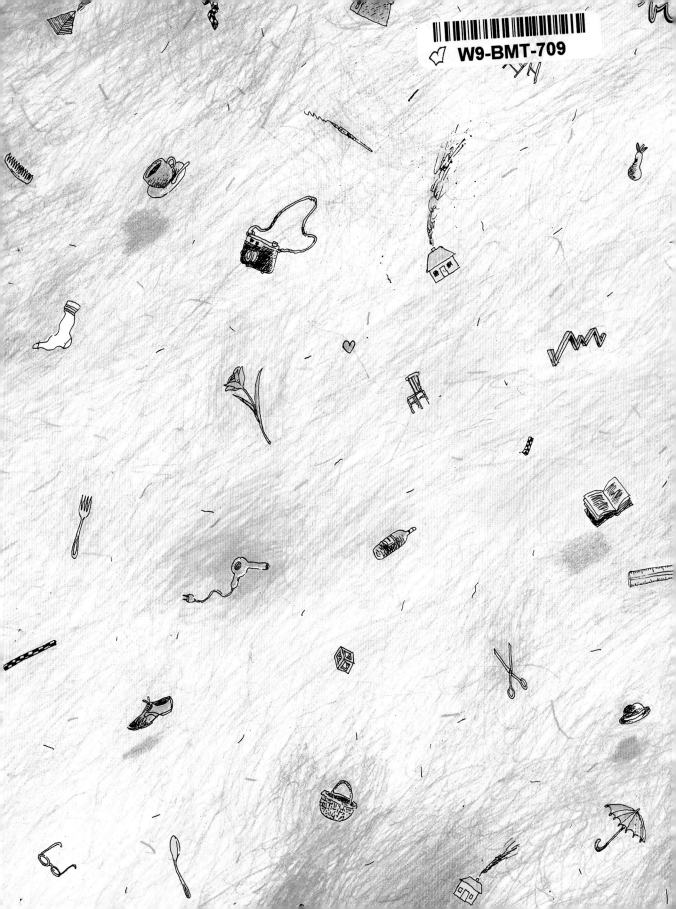

HENRIK DRESCHER

MacAdam/Cage Children's Books

The Strange Appearance of Howard Cranebill

Library of Congress Cataloging-in-Publication Data

Drescher, Henrik.
  The strange appearance of Howard Cranebill / by Henrik Drescher.
      p. cm.
  Summary: Having long wished for a child, Mr. and Mrs. Cranebill are
delighted with the baby they discover on their doorstep even though he
has an unusually long and pointy nose.

  ISBN 1-59692-134-X (hardcover : alk. paper)
  [1. Storks—Fiction. 2. Babies—Fiction.] I. Title.
  PZ7.D78383St 2005
  [E]—dc22
                              2005011623

MacAdam/Cage Children's Books
155 Sansome Street, Suite 550
San Francisco, California 94104
www.macadamcage.com

Printed in China.
1 2 3 4 5 6 7 8 9 10

For Joakim

Mr. and Mrs. Cranebill lived all alone in a little house with a pear tree in the backyard.

Their biggest wish was to have a child, and one morning when they opened their door they found a basket at their feet, with a little baby lying in it, all wrapped up.

The Dog

When they unwrapped the child they saw that it had sparkly eyes, a plump little belly, and an unusually long and pointy nose.

The baby was taken to the most accomplished overgrown-nose doctors, who felt, measured, looked, and poked at him for many hours.

They were distressed to admit that they had never seen a nose *that* long and pointy before. Further, they knew no cure for it.

So Mr. and Mrs. Cranebill ignored
the nose, named the baby Howard,
and proceeded to hug and cuddle him
as parents are supposed to do.

When Howard started to crawl he had to be helped out of some pretty nosey situations, like being stuck in the wall, or...

...getting tangled up at the zoo.

He had a lot
of trouble with
doughnuts,

and he always seemed to be dipping
his nose into the wrong things.

Howard liked to
climb and hide.

One day, when no one was looking,
Howard crawled into the backyard and
started climbing the big pear tree.

He had to be helped down.

A few days later Howard climbed even farther, and a ladder was needed to get him down.

During supper Howard's mind was on the
pear tree.

That night, after
Mr. and Mrs. Cranebill
were asleep, Howard
crept out his window
and headed for the
garden.

The next morning Mr. and Mrs. Cranebill were awakened by high-pitched singing in the garden. They went out, sleepy-eyed, to investigate.

There at the top of the pear tree sat little Howard, singing to a beautiful stork.

Even with their tallest ladder, the fire
department couldn't reach him.

Mr. and Mrs. Cranebill called and cried
to Howard, but he was too comfortable to
come back down.

Howard stayed in the pear tree for
many days and nights.

One morning Mrs. Cranebill looked
up and saw that Howard had changed.

His arms had become feathery wings
and his chubby little legs had changed
into long, graceful stork legs.

The unusually long and pointy nose
didn't seem out of place anymore.

AT DUSK they FLEW

That afternoon, every stork gathered to sing a
farewell song to Mr. and Mrs. Cranebill. At dusk they
left in small groups, flying south for the winter as storks
do each year.

The last to leave the pear tree was Howard. He
flapped his newly formed wings through the night air
and soon joined the other birds on their long journey.

Mr. and Mrs. Cranebill were sad to say good-bye to their son Howard, but they knew he would return the following spring, to build his nest in the tall pear tree in the backyard.

The End